A NOTE TO PARENTS

When your children are ready to "step into reading," giving them the right books is as crucial as giving them the right food to eat. **Step into Reading Books** present exciting stories and information reinforced with lively, colorful illustrations that make learning to read fun, satisfying, and worthwhile. They are priced so that acquiring an entire library of them is affordable. And they are beginning readers with a difference—they're written on five levels.

Early Step into Reading Books are designed for brand-new readers, with large type and only one or two lines of very simple text per page. **Step 1 Books** feature the same easy-to-read type as the Early Step into Reading Books, but with more words per page. **Step 2 Books** are both longer and slightly more difficult, while **Step 3 Books** introduce readers to paragraphs and fully developed plot lines. **Step 4 Books** offer exciting nonfiction for the increasingly independent reader.

The grade levels assigned to the five steps—preschool through kindergarten for the Early Books, preschool through grade 1 for Step 1, grades 1 through 3 for Step 2, grades 2 through 3 for Step 3, and grades 2 through 4 for Step 4—are intended only as guides. Some children move through all five steps very rapidly; others climb the steps over a period of several years. Either way, these books will help your child "step into reading" in style!

To Robert E. Howard, modern mythmaker
—M.C.

Text copyright © 1997 by Marc Cerasini. Illustrations copyright © 1997 by Isidre Mones.
All rights reserved under International and Pan-American Copyright Conventions.
Published in the United States by Random House, Inc., New York, and
simultaneously in Canada by Random House of Canada Limited, Toronto.

http://www.randomhouse.com/

Library of Congress Cataloging-in-Publication Data
Cerasini, Marc A., 1952–
The twelve labors of Hercules / by Marc Cerasini ; illustrated by Isidre Mones.
p. cm. — (Step into reading. Step 3 book)
SUMMARY: A simplified retelling of the adventures of the strongest man in ancient Greece
who has been given twelve "impossible" tasks to perform.
ISBN: 0-679-88393-2 (pbk.) — ISBN: 0-679-98393-7 (lib. bdg.)
1. Heracles (Greek mythology)—Juvenile literature.
2. Hercules (Roman mythology)—Juvenile literature. [1. Heracles (Greek mythology).
2. Hercules (Roman mythology). 3. Mythology, Greek. 4. Mythology, Roman.]
I. Mones, Isidre, ill. II. Title. III. Series. BL820.H5.C47 1997 393.2'0938'02—dc21 97-10010

Printed in the United States of America 10 9 8 7 6 5 4 3 2 1

STEP INTO READING is a registered trademark of Random House, Inc.

Step into Reading®

THE TWELVE LABORS OF
HERCULES

By Marc Cerasini

Illustrated by Isidre Mones

A Step 3 Book

Random House 🏠 New York

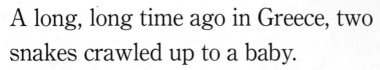

A long, long time ago in Greece, two snakes crawled up to a baby.

But the baby wasn't scared.

He just laughed and picked the snakes up. Then he squeezed them as if they were toys. The baby was so strong that he squeezed the snakes to death!

Who was that amazing baby?

His name was Hercules.

When Hercules was older, he started training to be a soldier. He learned how to use swords and spears.

He learned how to use a bow and arrow.

And he learned how to wrestle.

Hercules was very good at fighting. But it was hard for him to control his amazing strength. He was so strong that sometimes he hurt people when he didn't mean to.

One day Hercules went to fight a gang
of bandits. He beat them all in one battle!

Now Hercules was a hero. But he did not know what to do next.

Hercules went to the oracle to ask for help. The oracle was an old woman who could speak to the gods. She thought for a long time before she spoke.

"Go to the city and do twelve labors for the king," the oracle told Hercules.

Hercules was surprised. Everyone feared and hated the king. But the oracle was very wise, so away Hercules sailed.

Now, the king already did not like Hercules. He did not like anyone to be stronger than he was.

When Hercules arrived in the city, the king was ready for him.

"Go kill the Nemean Lion," he said to Hercules.

Hercules followed the lion's footprints to a dark cave in the woods. He drew his sword and entered.

The lion charged!

Hercules stabbed the monster, but his sword broke.

Hercules wrestled the lion to the ground. He squeezed it until it was dead. Then he skinned the lion and wrapped the fur around himself.

One task down, eleven to go!

"I must think of something more difficult," thought the king.

So he sent Hercules to kill the Hydra. The Hydra had nine heads. And if one was cut off, two more grew in its place!

Hercules went into the Hydra's swamp.
He set fire to his spear and waved it
around.

With a loud shriek, the Hydra attacked.

Hercules quickly cut off one head with his sword. Then he burned the neck with his flaming spear before the new heads could grow. He kept doing this until the Hydra lay dead at his feet.

Hercules dipped an arrow into the
monster's poisonous blood and saved it.
He might need it for another task.

Two tasks down, ten to go!

The king was not happy when he saw
Hercules back at the palace gates.

"Get me the Stag with Golden Antlers!"
he shouted.

It took Hercules a whole year to find the stag. It was beautiful! Hercules could not bear to kill it. Instead, he caught it and gently lifted it onto his back.

Hercules carried the stag back to the king. Then he set it free.

Three tasks down, nine to go!

The king was furious.

"Since you are so kind to animals," he said, "bring me the Wild Boar!"

The king laughed to himself. He was sure he would never see Hercules again.

Hercules chased the boar into the mountains. The snow was deep and the wind was icy. Finally the boar fell in a snowdrift. Hercules picked it up and carried it back to the city.

Four tasks down, eight to go!

The king was not pleased. It took him a few days to think of another task.

The next task was not only hard, it was disgusting. The king ordered Hercules to clean out the royal stables in one day.

The stables were huge and filthy, and the horses were as mean as could be.

Strength alone would not be enough for *this* task.

Hercules woke before the sun god's chariot flew above the horizon.

He went and looked at the stables. Then he looked at the river. He smiled.

As the sun came up, Hercules threw rocks and trees into the river. This made the river change its course until it flowed right through the stables.

The mess was washed away!

Five tasks down, seven to go!

The king now had to spend all his time thinking up hard tasks for Hercules to do.

"I bet you can't kill the brass-beaked birds who live in the swamp where boats always sink and swimmers always drown," said the king one day.

"Yes, I can," said Hercules.

But he was worried. He had no idea how he was going to do it.

Hercules still didn't know what to do when he got to the swamp of the brass-beaked birds. He decided to ask Athena, the Goddess of Wisdom, for help.

Athena heard Hercules' plea. She came down from Olympus and brought Hercules a pair of magic bronze rattles.

"Shake them," she commanded. "The sound will frighten the birds."

Before Hercules could say "Thank you," Athena vanished.

Hercules shook the rattles.

The brass-beaked birds flew into the air. Hercules grabbed his bow and his arrows. He shot the birds down, one by one.

Six tasks down, six to go!

"It's a good thing I'm done with half these tasks," Hercules thought. "No matter what I do, the king isn't happy with me."

Sure enough, the king threw his crown at Hercules. Hercules started to think that maybe the king was a little crazy.

"Try this one," said the king. "Bring me the Great Bull that lives on Crete."

Hercules sailed until he came to the
island of Crete. He left his boat on the
shore and climbed the steep, rocky cliffs.

Hercules found the Great Bull under an olive tree.

The bull took one look at Hercules and charged.

Hercules jumped on the bull's back.
He grabbed its horns. Then he hung on for
dear life as the bull bucked and kicked.

At last, the bull was too tired to fight.
Hercules dragged it onto his boat and
returned to the king.

Seven tasks down, five to go!

Hercules wondered what the king
would ask him to do next.

This time, the king smiled a sly smile.

"Here's an easy task," said the king. "Steal the horses of King Diomedes of Thrace."

An easy task? Hercules wondered if the king was playing a trick on him. But he sailed off to Thrace.

King Diomedes was expecting
Hercules. He held a huge feast in his honor.
Hercules started to feel bad that he
was going to steal this nice king's horses.
Then a woman whispered into his ear.
"Our king knows that you are going to
steal his man-eating horses. He plans to
kill you while you sleep."
"How did he find out?" asked Hercules.
But the woman had disappeared.

Hercules acted as if nothing was
wrong. At midnight he went to his room.
But instead of going to bed, he climbed out
the window. He hid beside the stables until
everyone was asleep.

One by one, Hercules led the horses to
his boat, hidden by the shadows of the
night.

There were still three horses in the
stables when the sun god's chariot rose.
In that first light, a soldier saw
Hercules.

The soldier ran to King Diomedes, who told his army to attack Hercules.

The battle was terrible!

When it was over, Hercules had defeated the army and one of the horses had eaten King Diomedes.

Hercules took the horses to his city.

Eight tasks down, four to go!

Hercules hoped the king would be happy at last.

The king was shocked when Hercules appeared in his throne room.

"But I told Diomed—" he started. Then he shut his mouth tight.

Now Hercules *knew* that the king had betrayed him. But what could he do?

"Bring me the golden belt worn by the Queen of the Amazons!" said the king.

Hercules sighed. At least there were only four tasks left.

Hercules sailed to the Amazons'
city. The Amazons were mighty warrior
women. They had never been defeated in
battle—until Hercules arrived!

He sailed back to the city with the
Amazon Queen's golden belt.

Nine tasks down, three to go!

"Where have you been?" the king yelled. "The ogre has stolen my cows. Get them back!"

Hercules could tell the king was trying to get an extra task out of him.

"This will be the tenth task," he said.

"Fine!" shouted the king.

Hercules sailed to the ogre's island. There, in plain sight, were the royal cows. Also in plain sight was the ogre. And this ogre was not only huge, he had three heads and six arms!

But Hercules had a plan.

Hercules took out the arrow with the Hydra's poisonous blood on it. He put it in his bow and took aim.

Twang! The arrow sailed through the air, right into the ogre's evil heart. And that was the end of the ogre.

Hercules drove the cows onto the boat and set sail.

Ten tasks down, only two to go!

The king knew he had only two more chances to get rid of Hercules.

He sent Hercules to get three golden apples from the end of the Earth. The end of the Earth was very far away. There, the god Atlas held up the sky.

"Where can I find the magic tree with golden apples?" Hercules asked the god.

"Only I can pick those apples," said Atlas. "Hold up the sky and I'll get them for you."

So Hercules took off his lion skin and took the sky from Atlas' shoulders. It was the heaviest thing Hercules had ever held. Atlas smiled and waved as he set off. "Please hurry," Hercules called.

Hours later, Atlas returned with the apples in his hand.

"Why don't I take them to the king for you?" asked Atlas.

Hercules could tell Atlas was glad to be rid of the heavy sky. He also knew that if Atlas left now, he would never return.

"All right," said Hercules. "But it's a little cold. Just let me put my lion skin on."

Atlas took the sky from Hercules' back.

As soon as the weight was lifted, Hercules grabbed the golden apples and ran.

"Poor Atlas," Hercules said to himself. "He has the hardest job in the world. Thank the gods that it did not become mine!"

Eleven tasks down, one to go!

What would the last task be?

"I want a dog," said the king when
Hercules returned.

Hercules nodded. He just wanted this
task done so he could be free.

"Bring me Cerberus!" said the king.

Everyone in the throne room gasped.

Cerberus guarded the Underworld,
where the dead walked in shadow forever.

No one had ever gone there and
returned. But Hercules had to try.

He went into an underground tunnel. He followed it until he came to the River Styx. There, Charon, the boatman of the dead, was waiting for him.

Hercules gave Charon a coin to row him across to the Underworld.

The Underworld was a place of mist and shadows. Ghosts drifted all around. A dog's angry howls filled the air.

Hercules followed the howls to Cerberus.

Cerberus growled and bared his teeth.

With his great strength, Hercules was able to hold the dog's jaws shut. Then he wrestled Cerberus to the ground and wrapped him in chains.

Hercules returned the way he had come, taking Cerberus with him.

"Here's your puppy," Hercules said to the king. "Twelve tasks down, none to go!"

And with that he freed Cerberus.

"Come back," the king shouted after Hercules. "You have to get rid of this beast for me!"

But Hercules didn't even turn around.

Hercules went right to the temple.
He thanked the gods and goddesses for
helping him with his tasks.

Then he set off for a life of adventure
that people tell stories about to this day!